Rosanna and Owl

*For Sandra,
In admiration
of your good work!
Enjoy*

Robert Mohr

Robert Mohr

Illustrated by KM Forster

To Rosanna

Table of Contents

Learn the method and find your own path.

Simon Buxton – The Sacred Trust

Chapter One – First Meeting

Rosanna woke with a thrill. It was Saturday, the day of her eleventh birthday and the first time she had ever invited her whole class to her birthday. She, her mother and her grandmother had been preparing for two weeks. Besides the food, the cake and the treats, her father and grandfather had busied themselves in the background.

"We've hired three acrobats and a man with trained parrots who do tricks and talk," her father had announced a week earlier.

The day before the party, they put up decorations - streamers, helium balloons, a few party favours including very pretty kaleidoscopes. "I hope it goes ok," she thought while twisting a strand of her light brown hair and brushing the tips across her nose and lips. She leapt out of bed.

It should go well. Rosanna was always popular. Even when she was just seven, she had lots of friends at school and in her neighbourhood. Generous by nature, she was quick to offer a turn on her bike to a younger child, "Ah sure, you try it."

But she was just as quick to show off and compete with the boys. She could control a football as well as most of them her own age. As she sparred on the large green space across from her house and her long wavy hair flounced about her head, she worked the ball back and forth between her feet before she shot it around a challenger. "Jeez you're quick," Tommy Ryan exclaimed, left behind, flat-footed. She laughed in good humour and chased after the ball, drawing her opponent behind her. The boys didn't mind. It was Rosanna and they took her as one of them.

Her only worry on this day, her birthday, was her two very best friends, Rachel and Jenny. The three had been the closest friends as far back as pre-school. But as Rachel and Jenny grew older, they also grew apart and their differences made them argue and sometimes fight. Rosanna had to come between them many times lately to keep peace.

When they were younger, they were always playing at each other's houses in the same estate, and they often slept over. They especially loved popcorn and fudge brownies, which Rosanna's mother helped them make. They liked tossing the popcorn and catching it in their mouths. Jenny, a born athlete with perfect timing and balance, could catch even the trickiest toss. When Rachel threw a stray kernel, Jenny looked as though she were flying when she sprang for it, her long blonde hair stretching out behind her like wings. She'd land in a tumble of arms and hair wrapped around her and spring to her feet with the kernel between her lips. They all laughed as she unwound her hair and chewed the kernel. Rachel's clumsy tosses gave the other two girls their biggest challenges.

Rosanna was close behind Jenny, but Rachel was hopeless. She didn't have Jenny's balance, and her glasses made it harder for her to see the flying kernels. They giggled as the corn kernel bounced off her nose and she tried to catch it with her hands, crushing it before she shoved the bits into her mouth. Or she missed catching the popcorn altogether and it got stuck in her curly auburn hair. They loved their popcorn-toss game, and their buttery smiles glistened with the sheer joy of it.

Rachel's talent lay in making up dramas they acted out, sometimes set in exotic places like Persia and in times long ago. She had always read books and knew lots of stories; this made up for her clumsiness. For their dramas, they borrowed old clothes and jewellery from their mothers, from their aunts and even from their grandmothers, who had old strangely styled clothes – paisley pantaloons and draw-string shirts with balloon sleeves. They painted their faces for the different roles.

"Stop and state your business!" commanded the guard.

"My business is none of yours. Step aside scoundrel."

Rachel loved the word 'scoundrel' and used it whenever she could. Then there would be a sword fight and the cry of a great lady who commanded them to stop and not disturb the peace. The drama flew high and often broke down in peals of laughter. With courts and kings and fine ladies and feasts of brownies, the girls would spend a Friday evening during a sleepover in great high jinks.

Yet the years passed and the differences between Rachel and Jenny began to push them apart. Jenny became more involved in sports. She took the captain role of their primary school mixed soccer team. The teacher encouraged her and Jenny excelled at the game. Out of school, she took gymnastics classes, which made her so busy that she had less time for her friends after school and on the weekends. She became very popular and, as a result, less patient with

Rachel's bookish, clumsy ways.

She started to make fun of Rachel behind her back and even in front of her with other children around. This horrified Rosanna, who was Jenny's equal and able to stand up to her and make her stop. Rachel withdrew more and more into her own world of books and fantasy. Her words were strong, so sometimes she'd make cutting remarks when she felt threatened.

"Oh yes, she's very athletic. Plenty of muscle between her ears," she'd say behind her back.

And to her face, "Let's see how long you can stand on one foot and bounce a football on your head."

"You can't even stand on one foot without falling on your ugly face." The bad feelings had grown impossible of late, and Rosanna worried they might spoil the mood of the party.

"They both *have* to be there. If only they will behave, it'll be perfect," she thought as she slid out of bed.

Downstairs, her father was preparing a special pancake breakfast with sweet strawberries, lemon and sugar, and real maple syrup, her favourite. As she ate, they all talked about the day ahead.

"The guests arrive at 2 o'clock, the performance starts at 2.30. We'll have food and cake after that," her mother recited. "And the weather is perfect today," her grandmother remarked.

The doorbell began ringing right on 2 o'clock, and the house and back garden filled with laughing children running about. During the show, everyone especially liked the antics of the parrots – their clever tricks and croaky voices answering questions.

"How many fingers?" the man asked. "Tree," answered the yellow-head Amazon.

Before they all dug into the food, Rachel was telling Rosanna and a small group of girls how much she loved the robin in *The Secret Garden*.
"Especially when he shows Mary the gate key. That was the best part." Jenny heard her and shot "bookworm" across the garden. That started the argument.

"What do you know? You can barely read," shot back Rachel.

"Four-eyes," barked Jenny, who had crossed the garden. She pushed Rachel so she fell backwards on the grass. The two girls glared at each other, daggers flying from their eyes and each ready to claw and scratch even though Rachel was no match for Jenny. Everyone froze.

Rosanna stepped between them and pulled Rachel up.

"Stop it you two! This is my birthday and I forbid you to fight." Because it *was* her day, they both stopped, but the bad feeling cast a shadow over the rest of the party. The two girls' bad feelings made everyone uncomfortable.

The next day, Rosanna visited her grandparents at their 2-story ivy-covered cottage in the Wicklow mountains. They had lived there so long that it had their own special smell of cooking, open wood fires and some curious smell like lavender or sage. She had her own bed upstairs for when she slept over. Its window looked out over her favourite meadow where she often played.

In mid-afternoon after lunch, she wandered into the meadow, thinking about her party and her friends. The long grass brushed against her hands and she pulled some seed tops off and shot them into the air like darts. "It was a perfect party if it weren't for Jenny and Rachel fighting," she thought. "It nearly spoilt the day. How am I going to fix this?"

She wished she could make them like each other again, but they were so completely different. Instead of laughing at each other's differences the way they used to, they got on each other's nerves. "Oh it's impossible!" she sighed.

She sat on her favourite large flat stone at the edge of the meadow and watched it starting to come back to life after its winter sleep. The long grasses were the first, and the wildflowers were heavy with buds. Soon they would all burst into bloom and the meadow would turn into a colourful carpet. "It's so beautiful. I wish I felt better and could enjoy it," she thought.

While she stared out over the grasses waving in a gentle breeze, a dragonfly distracted her thoughts as it hovered over an early thistle just in front of her. It landed so close she could study its shiny orange back glittering in the sunlight. Its wings looked like fine lace curtains. As she gazed at the beautiful creature, both the dragonfly and the plant seemed oddly large. "Or am I smaller?" She couldn't tell. "What a strange feeling." A large, loud honey bee flew past, its buzz filling her ears.

Before she could make sense of her confusion, a large Owl appeared from nowhere and stood several feet away. It ambled over to her. Its amber eyes shone sharp but wise and kind. Its feathers glistened brown with streaks of black and touches of butter cream. It was nearly her own size but she felt no fear. "How can this be?" she wondered. She curiously trusted him without question. The Owl stood still and waited for her to do something, so she stood up to face him.

"I'm Rosanna," she said to break the silence. "Who are you?"

He said nothing at first but waddled sideways so that he stood beside her.

"I am Owl," he hooted and the hooting formed clear words in her mind. "I've come to show you something that might cheer you up."

"How does this large creature know what I feel, and how can it speak so I understand?" Rosanna wondered. Even as these questions flitted through her mind, she also understood by the silence after the Owl spoke and by where it stood that it was inviting her to climb onto its back. She hesitated only for a moment before she leapt up over its wing shoulder and stood on its back. She took hold of two feather shafts on the back of its neck. This all seemed perfectly natural to her, that she had grown so small and she had just leapt onto the Owl's back. She tightened her grip and nuzzled into its neck. The soft feathers tickled her nose and she wiped it against her sleeve.

With a single flap, the Owl sprang from the ground and rose high above the meadow, high above the forest beyond. Rosanna held tight to the feather shafts and looked down. A wave of dizziness rushed through her head and stomach from this height, but she held her grip. The meadow looked like a turquoise lake and the forest a dark emerald shore. Her grandparents' cottage roof and gardens below looked small and the wind was stronger up in the sky. She clung to the Owl's feathers and crouched close to its body while her first fear left her in the wind.

The Owl tilted downwards toward the forest and plunged into the trees, flying at speed between the trunks, weaving and dodging. Getting used to this movement, Rosanna stood steadily on Owl's back and held to the feather shafts while the wind whipped through her hair, making it stretch straight out behind her. She bent one leg and then the other as the Owl tipped from side to side. She heard the wings slicing the air and the wind whistled in her ears.

The power of the Owl flowed up into her arms and raced all through her body. She felt perfect balance as they sped deeper into the forest.

They came to a clearing and the Owl dropped lower, tilted its wings, slowed to a stop and landed. Rosanna let go of the feather shafts and slid off its back to the ground. She grew again to her full height. As her size changed back to normal, she realized, "I was the one who shrank and not everything else that grew bigger." She felt a little dizzy at first but quickly adjusted to the change and then felt steady.

She looked around her. At the centre of the clearing stood a wide circle of boulders and, in the middle of this circle, a fire pit had gone stone dead. She climbed onto a boulder and stared at the dark, empty pit, her chin nestled in her hand. The Owl stood to the side and behind her, just out of sight.

"Why have you brought me here?" she wondered aloud.
"Watch," hooted the Owl.

In the corner of her eye, a shape moved. A man dressed all in green stepped out of the thick forest carrying a twiggy branch. He trotted in short steps towards the fire pit and placed it in the middle. As soon as the branch touched the ground, it burst into flame. At the same time, other figures stepped from the forest also carrying branches. Men, women, children appeared, even dogs who leapt excitedly beside the children, barking and trying to bite their sticks. Everyone carried twigs and branches to the fire and tossed them in. Soon a huge dancing flame lit the whole clearing. Rosanna barely noticed that it had become night all around her, making the fire brighter.

A young girl about Rosanna's age and height walked over to her and held out her hand. "Come join us."

Rosanna took her hand and together they skipped into the circle of forest people, who now pranced around the fire, laughing and shouting and singing songs with strange words. The tinkling of bells and the thrum of little drums wove into their singing and the crackling fire. Rosanna thrilled to the group's cry as an older boy flew through the flame in a great leap. The thrill felt like the power that ran up her arms when she held onto Owl's feathers in their flight. She joined the round dance, her face reddening with the heat of the fire, her voice rising with the others singing words she had never heard before. They made sense to her even though they had no meaning.

"They sing of a fresh stream and ferns growing beside it," she thought. "They feel like a birthday party without trouble. They feel like freedom." Round and round they danced until she was exhausted.

She squeezed the girl's hand and let go so she could step outside the circle for a moment. "I need to rest and collect my thoughts." She wondered how she could feel close to these forest people so quickly, like friends she had always known, almost like family. "It feels like a place I once knew, like another home, yet strange like a dream," she thought.

She saw the Owl standing between two boulders, watching her. She waved; he blinked. Encouraged, Rosanna skipped back into the circle and again found the girl's hand. As they skipped around the fire, no words passed between them yet she thought, "This is my sister."

Still, this wasn't really her home and family. "Home is where my bed is with its soft pillow and warm covers, where my mother and father are, where all my grandparents, my aunts, uncles and cousins know me and love me. This feels real, but it's a different world, not ordinary, not home." She knew she was a visitor and couldn't stay, no matter how exciting it was and how happy it made

her feel.

The Owl waddled close to the dancing circle and stood waiting. She knew it was time to go. She squeezed the girl's hand in farewell and skipped away from the dance. She shrank to a quarter the Owl's size and hopped onto his back. As they sprang from the ground and she held tight to his feathers, she felt a pang of sorrow. Part of her wanted to stay. She looked back to the fading speck of light and her wish to stay pulled at her heart. But her heart also beat in a steady rhythm calling her back home.

Owl flew through the forest by the same path they had come, darting between trees as Rosanna held tight to his feathers. He flew high over the forest into the sunlight and over the turquoise meadow and then made slow circles back down to the ground where they had started. Rosanna slid off and stood beside him for a moment, beaming with gratitude for being taken on such an adventure.

"Oh, Owl," she exclaimed, "Part of me wanted to stay there forever. Is that wrong? What if I did? What if I never came back?"

"That feeling is natural, Rosanna," his voice hooted low in her ears. "But I wouldn't let you get lost. I'll always bring you back. You can *visit* that other place any time you like."

"How can I do that? Will you take me there again?"

"We could go back into the forest again, but I'll take you to other places where you'll meet creatures who have something else to show you. Would you like that?"

"Oh yes!"

"Tell me. Do you feel better? I see the cloud is gone."

"I was worried about my two very best friends, who have stopped liking each other and now always argue. I would like to stop the bad feeling between them, but I can't and it makes me sad. The forest and its people made me feel better. I think my friends would get on again in that world. I'd like to bring them here so they could feel this."

"Yes, you do bring back something good, but keep it for yourself for now. You might be able to use it later."

"Owl, I want to see more. How can I find you again?"

"I'll come to you again when you're ready. For now, just hold this visit close to your heart. Keep it safe until you know more."

As he finished hooting these words, she grew to her normal size and the Owl seemed to shrink. Sitting down on the flat stone where they had met, Rosanna rested her elbow on her knee and settled her chin in her palm. Owl ambled away. She watched him spring into the air and rise in wide circles higher and higher in the blue sky until he became just a speck and disappeared.

She looked down and saw a large feather in the grass beside her. She picked it up. Light and dark brown streaks coloured its entire length, softened by touches of butter cream.

"Ah Owl," she said as she pressed it to her heart, closed her eyes and remembered her flight to the magic fire. "When will I see you again?"

Chapter Two – Visit to a Flower

Rosanna wandered into her favourite meadow near her grandparents' cottage in the mountains. It was already late spring, and during school breaks she loved to spend time at her grandparents'. They let her wander as she liked because it was safe here. She felt happy with the warm sunshine on her back as she walked. She took a deep breath and slowly blew it out, thinking, "Even the trouble between Rachel and Jenny seems far away here. I love this meadow."

She walked past her favourite flat stone at the edge of the meadow and towards the centre, where the grass grew tall and tickled her legs. Everywhere thousands of wildflowers were opening – blue and yellow, orange and red dabs of colour dotted the entire meadow.

"It's so beautiful," she burst out.

She stopped walking and listened to the buzzing of hundreds of bees; their hum made her dreamy. She settled on a large stone warmed by the sunshine and listened to the drone of the bees as they flew from flower to flower. The flowers nodded with their weight and sprang upright when they flew off. Just in front of her gaze, a white butterfly with a few black specks flitted over the tops of several open flowers, landing on each for a quick sip. A dragonfly whirred past her head, "just like the one I saw when I first met Owl," she thought. She watched a few of the flying insects nearest to her.

"I wonder what they find in the flowers and where they go afterwards."

She heard the sound of his wings before she saw the Owl. He landed a little distance to her right and waddled over. He looked into her eyes and brought her slowly out of her drowse.

Rosanna jumped up and exclaimed, "Owl, you're back!"

"Yes Rosanna," he hooted in his strange clear voice. "And I see you're enjoying the meadow springing back to life."

"It's beautiful. All the wildflowers are opening and the bees and butterflies are having a wonderful time. Just what are they up to?"

"Two things. They're busy feeding from the flowers and gathering food for their families. *And* they are spreading life as they go from flower to flower. Would you like to see what's really going on at the centre of these flowers? Are you ready for another visit?"

"Oh yes, but how can I do that? I'm way too big to go inside a flower."

Owl's eyelids narrowed over his bright amber eyes. It was his way of smiling. "Well, you know how big and small work in the *other* place. You already have one foot in there now. You just need to move the other foot in and you can be any size you wish."

Rosanna stood up beside Owl, excited by the chance to explore inside a flower. He turned to a bright orange poppy bud that was just starting to stand upright and not yet open.

Owl cooed softly to the bud. Its stem straightened completely and the bud began to tremble. She heard a little 'pop' as its cover opened and the petals of the poppy began to open. Bright coral petals unfolded into a multi-petal cup, black at its centre and little hair-like stalks standing from the middle. Rosanna gasped at its beauty. "It's getting bigger!"

It grew larger and larger, showing her more of its detail: the little hairs on its stem, the streaks of colour inside its petals. Soon it towered over her high in the blue sky. As she looked around, she saw that everything was larger than she and Owl.

"Let's explore," Owl invited.

She hopped onto his back and he flew into the air above the meadow . He made several downward spirals towards the flower, which grew so large that Rosanna could see nothing else but its colour. They landed on the edge of an enormous petal like two tiny poppy seeds. Rosanna slid off Owl's back onto the surface of the petal, her feet sticking to its steep slope. She inhaled its bitter-sweet scent and its deep coral tones filled her eyes.

"Oh my! It's so different close-up," she exclaimed as she took a few careful steps on the ribbed surface of the petal. "It's solid but soft to walk on." It was sticky enough that she trusted she wouldn't slip and slide down its steep slope into the centre.

From the centre, one huge round stalk rose high as a great pine tree. Many slender stalks grew in a circle around it, and each had dusty yellow pads at the tops. Rosanna stared at them as she stood at the same height on the flower petal. "They're bigger than my bed."

Owl explained, "Those pads are covered with sticky pollen, which the flying insects love, especially the bees. They use it to make their hives and honey."

Just then a golden honey bee, already dusty from other flowers, landed on top of a group of the pads across from her and began scooping more pollen into little cups on her legs. The whole flower leaned and swayed with the bee's weight. Rosanna gripped the edge of the petal so she wouldn't fall off and adjusted herself for a better view. She

watched the bee loll in the pollen with such pleasure that it made her giggle.

"She really loves it, doesn't she?"

"Yes, she does. And watch what happens next."

The bee crawled over the tops of the pollen stalks until her cups were overflowing. As she took off with a heavy buzz, hundreds of pollen grains spilled from her cups. They rained down upon Rosanna and Owl and stuck to the slope of the petals. Some also landed on the top of the big centre stalk. Her feet stuck a little as she took a few steps.

"It's so sticky! Why does the flower make all this pollen?" Rosanna asked shaking it out of her hair and brushing it off her arms and shoulders.

Owl tilted his head and looked at her. He answered without blinking. "Hoo, that's the great magic at the heart of the flower. Pollen is half of what the flower needs to make new flowers. We're at the door of the other half. Let's fly to the top of the big stalk to see what's happening there."

Rosanna mounted Owl's back, and up they flew to the top of the glistening tower. They landed on its bumpy surface, which was covered with little hairs and cup-like flaps. Some of the pollen grains had nestled inside those flaps.

"What a strange place," exclaimed Rosanna. She peered more closely at one of the little flaps. She saw how a pollen grain fit perfectly into its shape, like an egg in an egg cup. She pushed it with her foot to see if it would move. It stayed fast in place.

"It won't budge. And it's hard like a thick egg shell."

As she spoke, something began to happen to the pollen shell. It started to crack and break open. Out of it a tube began growing straight downwards through the big stalk towards the centre of the flower. Rosanna could see right through everything as if it were all clear. She saw a tiny seed drop from the shell and into the tube and then start sliding downwards.

"Let's follow the seed," said Owl.

Shrinking even smaller, they both squeezed into the long green tunnel and started sliding down after the pollen seed. Rosanna could see it just beneath them filling the entire passageway. The passage was moist and green light shone through the walls.

They slid the rest of the way down and out of the tube. They stood inside a tiny pod beside a large egg. A small crack had formed on the surface of the egg where the seed landed. It made a sharp sound as the crack opened wider and the seed dropped through it into the egg's centre. She watched the seed melt into the egg as they become one. The tube broke away from the surface of the egg and the opening sealed over again.

"Now that the pollen and egg have come together, Rosanna, the egg will start to grow into a plant seed. When it's ready, it will fall from the flower to the ground, or a bird or the wind will carry it away and drop it somewhere else, perhaps very far from here. If all goes well, the seed will sprout into a new plant. This is what all the plants around us are doing with the help of the bees and others, making new plants to fill the meadow with flowers."

Rosanna's eyes grew wide as Owl's. She walked towards the egg and placed both hands on its surface. It was warm and she felt it vibrating. She stepped back and gazed at it for a long time to remember all she was seeing.

Owl startled her with a nudge. It was time to go. They slid back up into the moist tube and rose to the top of the main stalk. From there they jumped onto one of the pads at the top of a slender stalk, where more pollen grains loosened and rained down onto the flower petals. Some floated away in a gentle breeze. As they leapt to the surface of a huge petal, they grew to the size of poppy seeds again. Rosanna looked around, filling her memory with the shapes and the colours of the flower – the huge centre stalk, the filaments with their pads of pollen, the bright coral of the petals, the lovely scent of it all. Without a word, she climbed onto Owl's back and up they flew in wide circles high above the poppy. They made three downward spirals and landed in the long grass beside the stone where Owl found her day-dreaming before. She slipped off his back.

"Thank you Owl for showing me the inside of the poppy. It was wonderful to grow tiny and to see the bee work and the pollen drop inside the egg. I feel as I've been very, very far away. After this, I'll never look at flowers and bees the same way again. Thank you!"

Owl swivelled his head towards her and his eyelids narrowed as he looked gently into her wide, sparkling eyes. "You are most welcome Rosanna. Give yourself a few days for this to sink in and then you'll see me again. Goodbye for now."

He turned and ambled away into the grass, made a single leap and flew in great wide circles up into the sky until he disappeared from her sight. She smiled, stood up and gazed at the poppy she had just visited. Then she turned to walk back to her grandparents' cottage, musing over her visit to the flower.

Chapter Three – Meeting Otter

Rosanna's mind was full of worry about Jenny and Rachel, who had argued terribly again during a break at school. This time it was about Rachel's clothes, which Jenny called 'frumpy'. "They were actually 'blousy'," Rosanna thought, "and looked like they belonged to another age." Rachel liked to imagine herself living in other times such as the late 1800s. She really did have a good sense for clothes, just different from everyone else's.

Rachel retorted to Jenny's remark, "You have no style at all, ball girl. Shouldn't you be out on the football pitch running in circles?" It was true that Jenny always dressed in sportswear and had no time for feminine frills. She looked just right as she was. They both did. Yet their unpleasant exchange deeply upset Rosanna. She felt like giving up any hope of saving their friendship.

She wandered along aimlessly near her grandparent's cottage in the late afternoon, skirting her favourite meadow and trudging along a dirt road up the hill towards the dense forest. Everything cast long shadows, especially the old leafless oak tree at the top of the hill. She shaded her eyes and followed the tree's shadow from her feet up the trunk to its branches, where she spotted Owl looking down at her. He could see she was upset. He ruffled his feathers.

"What troubles you, Rosanna?" he hooted.

"Oh Owl, my two dear friends had a big argument at school today and said outright that they hated each other. Rachel is very clever but normally quiet and shy. Jenny is loud and funny but she has a wicked tongue and teases Rachel. Rachel is afraid of Jenny' strength, so she uses words to hurt her back. I can't be with the two of them together because they dislike each other so. They fight and I feel torn between them. It's very confusing and I don't know what to do."

He glided down to her in one small circle. He looked into her darkened eyes and said, "I see you feel you should fix this but you are too close to it. You need some lightness and distance to help you escape the trap you're in. I'd like you to meet someone who might help. It's far away but I think you'll enjoy the visit. We have to cross an ocean and a continent."

"Oh I couldn't possibly do that and be home for supper," she protested even as she took a little step towards him.

"Trust me. It won't take long. And it might help you to feel better."

"Yes Owl. Who is this person?"

"He's not really a person; he's a sea otter. There is no better cure for a heavy heart than Otter."

Rosanna shrank and leapt onto Owl's back. He sprang into flight high over the forest and sped towards the west. The air whistling through Rosanna's hair and past her ears seemed no stronger than it had before, but the land passed more swiftly beneath them until they came to the edge of a great ocean.

They glided close to the surface so she could hear the rush of water breaking at the peaks of huge rolling waves. Rosanna saw ships in the distance pass by quickly. They slowed their flight for a moment as the huge body of a whale broke the surface of the water and sent a beautiful rainbow spray into the sunlight. On they sped. It seemed less than a minute till they came to land again. Owl rocketed across plains and over mountains until he carried them to another coastline, where the breakers crashed against the shore.

They landed near the opening to a large cave but Rosanna stayed on Owl's back, feeling uncertain about this new place. Smooth rocks reached out into the water to form many tide pools, and the surging waters washed over them, filling the pools and spilling out again. Near a calm area beside a cluster of rocks, Rosanna caught sight of a head that poked from under the water and disappeared.

A little distance away, where a small river emptied into the ocean, she saw the head again as it poked from the water. This time it stayed up and glided towards the mouth of the river. Owl flew the short distance and landed on a flat rock nearby. The otter floated on his back, holding his paws folded on his chest. His face had a funny expression.

"Is he smiling at us?" she asked as she slid off Owl's back.

"I think he is. Go ahead. He's friendly enough," Owl assured her.

She walked into the water towards the otter. Their eyes met and, though the water was cold, she felt warmth fill her body. The otter turned over, and she straddled his back without a word. She leaned forward and hugged his body with her arms and legs till she felt secure. Then he dived beneath the surface. She could see the waving seaweed and fish darting about in the crystal clear water. She found she could still breathe.

The otter swam away from the shore, past the breakers and towards the mouth of a large bay. Above the surface, Rosanna could see a great orange bridge arching over the mouth of the bay as they entered it. She thought she had seen it before in pictures. They sped between a city and a small island until they came to the far shore, where they swam among enormous ships of grey steel. Rosanna saw men and cranes above the surface moving huge containers on and off the ships. It all looked very serious and a bit rough.

Suddenly, they flew out of the water and over the top of one ship in a great arc of rainbow mist, surprising the workmen, who stopped working and pointed up at them. As they plunged back into the water, they both laughed, the Otter in a high-pitched bark that Rosanna could hear even under water. This put them in a jolly mood as they sped back out into the bay, past large sharks who eyed them suspiciously.

They returned to the shore some distance from the ships. Rosanna climbed off the otter's back and he padded out of the water. At first he seemed awkward on land, but then he stood up straight to the height of a full-grown boy, upright and agile, yet still an otter. She stared for a moment, smiled, and said, "I'm Rosanna."

"Otter," barked the creature.

They began to walk through streets like mates, yet no one noticed them as though they were invisible.

"People see mostly what they expect to see," barked Otter. "They see only a boy and a girl. Making them see just what you want them to see is a trick you can practise." He winked. "Let's have some fun. I know a café."

In a twinkling, they arrived at the entrance to a busy café with a large outdoor terrace surrounding the central room. White posts and low railing fences defined the outdoor seating area, which was full of chatting people sipping coffee, tea and juices of all colours. The mixed fragrances reminded Rosanna of her grandparents' kitchen with the window open on a fine summer morning. Music floated from inside the café.

They sat on a bench seat along an outdoor wall at a table beside a large woman who sat at the next table. She wore a flowery dress and a large straw hat. She smiled warmly at them and said, "Hello", pretending not to notice that the boy was really an otter. Her eyes twinkled. As the café bustled around them, a glass of mango juice simply appeared before Rosanna, and Otter held a glass of green juice the colour of seaweed between his paws. The mango was so delicious that she drank it down in two lifts.

The woman looked at them again and smiled even more warmly, almost laughing with delight at seeing a girl and an otter sitting near her. Otter got up, walked over to her table and sat beside her on the bench. He barked softly and nudged his nose against the side of her huge bosom, waving a paw for Rosanna to do the same. Giggling, she stood up, walked to the other side of the woman and slid over to her on the bench. She nuzzled her nose, just as Otter, against the smiling woman's other breast. The big woman began to laugh.

Her laugh grew large and the ground began to tremble. The more joyously she laughed, the more the earth rumbled and the walls and posts began to shimmer as though under water. When she stopped laughing, everything settled back into solid shapes again. The woman inhaled deeply and then exhaled a great breath, fragrant as jasmine.

Everyone stopped whatever they were doing and stared in their direction, caught up in the shaking magic, their mouths open. But as soon as the laughing and shaking stopped, they continued chatting and sipping their drinks as if nothing had happened, as though they forgot it did. The air crackled and made Rosanna's body vibrate. The woman smiled at her with the warmth of a hundred grandmothers. It made Rosanna feel that everything was ok, and her earlier heavy mood completely lifted like mist from a lake at sunrise.

Rosanna and Otter stood up and, first bowing to the woman in the flowery dress and the great straw hat, they walked out of the café. They skipped merrily along the footpath laughing and found their way down the road towards the shore of the bay. Again it was a twinkling before they arrived.

"Owl was right," exclaimed Rosanna. "You *are* the best cure for a bad mood anyone could possibly wish. I think you could even fix my friends."

"There's one thing more," barked Otter. "First we must return to the cave where Owl is waiting for us." Already at the edge of the bay, Rosanna climbed onto Otter's back and, whoosh, they dived back into the refreshing water. Out past the suspicious sharks and the island and the city, out through the mouth of the bay and under the orange bridge, they swam and entered the great ocean. They came swiftly to where Owl perched on a leaning tree beside the river near the cave. Owl could see immediately that Rosanna's heavy mood had lifted. She nearly glowed.

"Oh Owl, we had the most wonderful time. We met a large woman in a café and ...."

But before she could continue her story, Otter stepped in front of her, held up one paw and began to dance. He rocked from side to side and patted his hind feet against the ground in a regular beat. He bobbed his head up and down in time with the rhythm of his feet. Rosanna became entranced and started to imitate his dance.

Then, the otter did the most extraordinary thing. He opened his mouth wide and wider still and leapt towards her, swallowing her in one gulp. She became tiny and felt she was falling in a small, dark, moist tunnel as she slid all the way down into his tail. There, she turned and then began to grow again. She grew to the exact size and shape of his body. In fact, she so filled his body that they became the same creature. She saw through his eyes and felt his nose as her nose. She felt his whiskers twitch, felt his paws scratch the sand and the warmth of his body as her own. To a silent rhythm beating deep inside her, she continued the dance the Otter had begun. She pat her feet against the ground in a regular beat. She swayed her body and head in a sloshing watery dance. The rhythm moved her with a force strong as the rumbling earth she'd felt and heard in the café when the great woman laughed. The taste of ripe berries filled her mouth, and she smelled jasmine again. She felt strong and happy and free as she danced and she danced.

Then the rhythm stopped and she stood still. She felt an urge to step forward and, as she did, she stepped right outside Otter's body and returned to her own shape. She turned to face him and looked into his twinkling eyes. She could say nothing aloud but mouthed the words, "Thank you."

He barked once and leapt into the river. He came up floating on his back, his forepaws folded contentedly on his chest, and paddled out to the open waters.

Rosanna turned and ran to where Owl perched on the leaning tree. "Oh Owl, I'm so happy you brought me here. We had a wonderful time. The strangest part came at the end. Did you see what happened?"

"Yes, and everything else too. The laughing woman, the dance and the Otter himself are all just for you Rosanna. No one can explain these things to you. You'll have to find your own understanding of them. Come. It's time to return home."

He flew down to her and she hopped onto his back. Fast as thought, Owl sped away from the cave at the edge of this ocean, across plains and over mountains until they came to the coastline of the other ocean, where the breakers crashed against the shore. Again while crossing, Rosanna spied ships in the distance, and the huge body of a whale broke the surface and sent a beautiful rainbow spray into the light of the sun. It seemed less than a minute before they came to the shore of her home. They flew to the hill of the bony old oak tree where they first met, landed and Rosanna hopped off Owl's back.

"Owl, I was sad because of the trouble between Rachel and Jenny, but now I feel so happy I could burst."

"Wonderful, but you don't have to do anything right away with this feeling Rosanna. Just hold onto it until our next meeting and see if it helps you with your trouble without your trying." With that he flew up into the tree, fluffed up his feathers and grew very still.

Rosanna turned and walked back down the hill towards her grandparents' cottage, wondering if she was late for supper. She looked back before turning a corner, but Owl was already gone. The sun was only a bit lower in the sky than when she began. She was not late. She smiled and sighed, "Owl."

Chapter Four – Your Pure Wild Heart

One hot summer day, Rosanna and Jenny went swimming in a small lake near her grandparents' cottage. They chatted as they lay at the sandy edge of the shore, drying in the sun. Rosanna asked, "Why do you hate Rachel so much, Jenny? We three used to be such good friends."

"Oh she's such a goggle-eyed nerd, always with her nose in a book, and she has no coordination. In sports class she couldn't even kick the football straight. She's useless!"

"But she's very clever. Have you even tried to talk to her lately?"

"Why bother? We don't like the same things, and besides, she hates me too."

Rosanna changed the subject, but she felt sad that Jenny dismissed their friend who had once been so close. It divided Rosanna's heart because she couldn't be with them both at the same time. She missed their trio.

She stayed on with her grandparents for a couple of days during a three-day school break. One afternoon, she took a walk deep into the woods beside her meadow, exploring beyond the familiar twists in the path that she knew almost blindfolded. She had got nowhere with Jenny and Rachel when she tried to pass Otter's joy over to them at school. "It simply won't pass over."

She came to a thicket of bushes and trees and spied an opening in the overgrowth she could just fit through. As she stepped closer, she heard a babble of water calling her. She didn't hesitate. She ducked in past the scraping bramble, not minding the tickle of spiders' webs against her face and arms. She pressed deeper into the thicket until she came to an opening, lit by green filtered light and high enough for her to stand upright. There she saw a little brook rushing about the rocks and dropping into small plunge pools.

"Oh how beautiful," she cried as her eyes adjusted to the leafy light. That's when she saw Owl perched on an old oak limb arching over the water. "Owl, did you bring me here?"

He ruffled his feathers and swivelled his head away. Then turned it back and stared into her eyes through his glowing amber eyes. "Yes," he said in her head. "I want to take you to meet a new creature, one very different from the laughing Otter who took you to play in a café.

Just then she saw another pair of amber eyes, very like Owl's but further apart and more piercing. The two fiery orbs stared at her from inside a holly bush. The hair stood on the back of her neck and arms. She froze. "Oh!"

"That, my child, is Panther. He is good but wild and strong. He can show you something you need to see, but you have to face him bravely."

The holly trembled, but still only the eyes shone from inside its shadows. Rosanna turned to face them, a bit frightened yet reassured by Owl's words. Her whole body tingled as it did when she flew with Owl. The Panther began to step out from the dark shadow, first a huge black paw and then the leg leading to his glistening chest and head. His head was huge, much bigger than seemed possible. When he stepped completely out of the bush, his face was higher than hers. Something calm in its eyes told her she was safe. She knew she couldn't run anyway. They stood facing each other without moving, eyes locked. Owl broke the silence.

"No one is Panther's friend. But he knows *you* already. The best way to know him is to become him as you did with Otter. Don't be frightened. Just relax."

The Panther circled around her twice, his soft tail sliding around her waist as he moved. His deep purrr filled her ears. He faced her silently for a moment. Then he stood to full height and placed his enormous paws on her shoulders. She felt no weight but the tingling energy increased. He opened his mouth wide, wider, and with a quick leap, he swallowed her whole from head to foot. It happened so quickly that Rosanna had no time to think about danger or Otter or anything other than sliding in moist darkness down towards the Panther's tail. At its tip, she turned and began to grow. She grew into the exact shape of his body until they were the same. She felt her feet and hands were his paws, her head his head. Only her hair still hung from the back of Panther's head. Her mind had changed too. She still thought her way but now she understood Panther's thoughts too, and they had no words. She translated.

"Run with me. We have something to do." They sprang and a path opened before them. She heard the flap of Owl's wings above and slightly behind. The feeling of paws lightly drumming the earth thrilled her, four of them rapidly – badababump...badababump – in a regular rhythm. The touch felt sure, powerful, quick. Through Panther's eyes, she saw everything with a new night vision. She saw all the leaves and branches and what was hidden inside the thickets. She saw mice scurry, insects freeze, leaves fall inside bushes from the force of their running.

The path rushed beneath them. Trees fallen over cave openings sprouted new shoots. Ferns uncurling towards the sun grew in large patches everywhere. She saw two huge dancing butterflies in a clearing over another stream, the sun glinting off their wings. Mostly, she felt the power of her body inside the Panther, her shoulder muscles tightening as she caught her weight, her hind muscles exploding as she sprang, stride after stride. His great beating heart sent waves of power through her, forcing out a huge air-splitting roar that flooded the forest with its sound. Even Owl lifted up in his flight from the force of the sudden roar.

"Where are we going," she wondered as she settled into his stride. "Who is this creature? What does Panther do?" A sharp turn to the right and a leap over a stream brought them to another thicket, denser than the one she had first entered. At the centre of it, she saw a wounded fawn, almost a yearling, her legs tangled in the branches. Her knees were bleeding and she had a deep cut on her hind leg. As they approached, Rosanna could see terror in the fawn's eyes. But she knew this was more from being trapped and from whatever drove the poor creature into the trap than from the Panther's sudden appearance.

Panther sat near the fawn's head to reassure her. Rosanna felt the calming effect he had on the frightened creature.

"She's nearly at the age of leaving her mother but not fully. While they were feeding in the meadow, her mother was shot by hunters. This little one fled in panic and got entangled here in this bramble. She's hurt and will die slowly if we don't free her."

As one, Panther and Rosanna stepped forward and, using powerful forepaws, spread the thick branches apart so the fawn could stagger out. She fell as she bolted into a clearing. Too frightened and too weak from her injuries to move, she held still as Panther walked up and stood over her. Rosanna felt a different energy gather inside her. A liquid, sweet and pure, filled her mouth. Saliva dripped from her mouth onto the fawn's wounds – head, knees and the deep cut on her hind leg. The fawn lifted her head, and quickly the wounds healed over. She made a clumsy effort to stand and face Panther but her legs folded beneath her.

She needed more strength. Again, Rosanna felt the energy gather inside her just before Panther breathed into the fawn's nostrils. A warm mist, full of the fragrance of a morning meadow and something like fresh milk, filled her throat. The fawn closed her eyes, raised her nose towards the panther's mouth and inhaled deeply. As she did, she seemed to grow a little and her white spots faded away. She became a full yearling in one breath. Panther backed away and the young deer leaped up and kicked her hind legs.

"Now she has no herd, no clan, so we'll introduce her to one nearby." Panther started padding down a forest path and the yearling followed close behind, every now and then making gleeful little leaps. The path opened onto a green meadow dotted with wildflowers. At the far end stood a small herd of does with several yearlings and a scattering of fawns. Panther led the young deer along the edge of this meadow towards the herd. Each magnificent doe lifted her head to watch their approach. Rosanna sensed they were not frightened and she wondered at this. "Later", she thought, "I'll ask Owl why Panther did not frighten the deer." When they stood ten feet from the largest doe, Panther growled deeply both his greeting and his request that they take in the young deer whose mother had been killed. Rosanna understood the thoughts between Panther and the doe. There were no words but a silent agreement passed between them.

The does gathered around the yearling and gave her gentle, welcoming nudges. The largest doe stood apart from the others, facing Panther in a silent thank you and farewell. Now Rosanna knew she didn't need to ask Owl why the deer weren't afraid of Panther. "Panther is a spirit, not a brute beast. I wonder if anyone other than the deer can see him."

The rescue completed and the yearling embraced by her new herd, Panther returned along the edge of the field and back again into the forest. He raced at full speed towards the place they had started. He ran even more wildly and some of his leaps felt like flying. Rosanna heard the airbrushing of Owl's wings overhead just before they arrived to the clearing where they had all met.

When they stopped, Panther stood to full height on his hind legs, so she could simply step forward out of his body. Owl landed in the oak tree beside where she stood next to Panther, her right hand on his back. She felt his warmth, his breathing and the sleek texture of his fur, a real live Panther. Owl watched her from the oak branch and asked, "What have you learned from meeting Panther?" She thought for a moment, eyes half closed, and when she looked up towards Owl, Panther was gone.

A little startled but getting used to such extra-ordinary events, she answered: "Panther is like Otter in some ways. I trusted them both even though they both did very strange things. Otter is playful while Panther is fierce. It was from his fierceness that I felt him heal the fawn, who had no fear of him. The healing juice came from a power inside him. I can't explain how, but I felt it happen."

"Yes, that's Panther. He knows everything and is pure. His wild heart makes the healing juice and the breath that healed the fawn."

Nothing more needed saying. Owl flew out of the opening in the thicket and Rosanna pawed her way through the branches. He flew upwards in widening circles and vanished just as she slipped out through the opening herself. She stopped and stared down at the ground, remembering her experience, wondering how it applied to Rachel and Jenny. But mostly she held it close to her heart, held close the Panther's pure wild heart.

Chapter Five – I want to go up!

Rosanna sat on a window seat upstairs in her grandparents' cottage, looking out over the Wicklow woods. The windows were swung wide open to the fresh summer morning air. She looked up into the blue sky dotted with huge white clouds. "I wish I could go up there and forget all this." She felt so frustrated over the trouble between her friends that she imagined herself sitting on one of those clouds, a princess on big fluffy cushions. Just then she heard the whoosh and Owl landed on the window sill beside her.

"Oh Owl," she cried out, "you're back. It seems so long since I last saw you." Owl ruffled his feathers, swivelled his head and looked deep into her eyes. His own amber eyes seemed especially bright, like fire shining through glass. She spoke first.

"Do you know what I wish?

"What's that, Rosanna?"

"I wish I could go up there, sit on one of those clouds and be Princess of the Sky! That would be truly grand."

"You want to go up? That *is* possible, but remember Rosanna, no matter how high you travel, you won't escape your problems. You might find some answers, but not escape. Hop on and I'll take you to where you can start."

Rosanna shrunk and hopped onto Owl's back, held two large pinions and off they flew, high over the forest to a large hill. They landed on the hilltop, from where she could see the valley and fields far below. Right away, she noticed two things: a ring of stones surrounding them where they landed and, just outside the ring, a craggy old thorn tree.

As she fixed her gaze on the tree, Owl explained, "That is an old Whitethorn, over 800 years by human count. They often grow in hedges, but now and then one outlives the others and stands alone as this 'Grandmother Thorn'. When they grow this old, it means the fairy folk have lived with them for many years and they have become powerful fairy trees. The stones around you form a fairy ring, where on full moon nights the little people dance beneath the moon. It is a special place. Come closer to the tree."

They walked towards the old thorn tree, and Rosanna saw a large hole in its trunk, big enough for her to fit her head and shoulders. "This is your way to the other world," said Owl. "Once you go in, you can move upwards or downwards. This time, go up and I'll meet you at the top. But first, ask Grandmother Thorn her permission." Owl disappeared.

Rosanna stepped back a little and, facing the whole tree, she said, "Grandmother Thorn, thank you for letting me come to you. May I enter you to go up and meet Owl?" She felt the tree tremble as if to say yes. She felt she was being welcomed, so she stepped forwards and placed her hands either side of the opening and slid in. She began to rise up inside the tree trunk, whose rings were like the ribs inside of a whale. She became smaller as she entered a branch, and smaller as she continued through a twig until she came to its tip. She popped out onto a small cloud that looked like a magic carpet made of woven mists. There sat Owl. She nestled beside him, each for the moment their natural size, or so it seemed. The cloud began to move in upward spirals, higher and higher between huge billowing white clouds. It passed through a hole that led to what looked like a stone staircase made of grey cloud. The cloud

carpet stopped beside the stairs, and Owl motioned with his wing for her to step onto them.

"Climb these stairs to see where they take you."

"Will they hold me?"

She stepped gingerly off the cloud onto the stairs, and they did hold her. Slowly at first, she began to trot up the hundreds of steps while Owl flew above her. The steady beat of her steps kept her from getting tired.

"I feel I could go on forever."

She grew stronger as she climbed until she came to a door on her right side, a massive wooden door that seemed to be made of the same stuff as the stairs. It was rough and wide. Its top was arched and the handle looked like black iron. She stopped and Owl landed on a step above her.

"Go ahead. Knock."

Three firm knocks and the door slowly opened without a sound. Before her stood a tall wisp of a man unlike any she'd ever seen. He seemed half made of cloud.

"Come in young lady," he said in a gentle, formal tone. She stepped into a room past the figure and made a complete turn to look around her. The floor and walls seemed to be solid stone. To the left, a long wooden table was covered with books, blank parchment, a few ink jars and quills, an hourglass and a large perch, where Owl flew and landed. He looked quite at home. Beyond the table, she saw an arched window that looked further into the sky and down to the earth below. To her right, she noticed a huge iron cauldron with a low fire beneath it. Something in it was bubbling hot, and it gave off a scent like mint mixed with freshly cut wood.

She turned to face the man, who stood at least seven feet tall. She felt no fear, only a respectful curiosity. He stroked his long wispy beard and studied her; his silvery eyes sparkled in amusement. He wore a long, midnight-blue robe covered with stars and crescent moons. It hung from his neck to his feet. Upon his head, he wore a long conical hat of the same blue material, also covered with stars. Rosanna felt more awe than humour. She cried out before she thought, "Merlin!"

"Close. My name is Merú, and you are most welcome here, Rosanna. I can see, however, that you seek something beyond this room. I shall take you to where you need to go."

And with that he opened his robe until it filled the room. Rosanna stepped forward into the space he opened. He closed the robe around her, and together they flew out the arched window and deep into space.

Through the robe, she could see stars in the distance; the planets were closer and much bigger. They flew past the Moon, past Mars, past the rings of Saturn until they went beyond the planets altogether. They sped towards a light that looked like a star but it quickly grew into the shape of a crystal palace illuminated by its own light.

They landed at the foot of a wide staircase, clear and lit from within like the rest of the palace and warm to her feet. She stooped down to touch it and felt it vibrating.

"You must go alone from here," said Merú folding his arms, closing his eyes and growing perfectly still.

Rosanna turned from him and began to climb the long staircase, just as she had climbed the stairs to the wizard's door before, in a rhythmic trot. She arrived at the top and faced a large room, open only at the end where she stood. At the far end sat a radiant woman in a light blue gown.

"Come forward Rosanna."

Her beautiful voice rang out and turned into a sound like one of her grandmother's singing bowls. She walked towards her without fear, noticing that this woman's hair and eyes gave off light and warmth just as the walls and floors did, only brighter. Her eyes had no colour but were pure light. Rosanna couldn't speak.

"I am pleased that you have come. I am your protector in life and have many different forms and names. Here, I am Glinn. I watch over you on your path as you seek truth and beauty. Although you do not know it yet, you have come for something I have to give you."

She took a small crystal vial from inside the folds of her gown. "This is a precious liquid, an *elixir*. It will revive the light in you when you have had too much darkness. It is a balm that will bring you back to health when you grow very sick. Taste a drop now so you know how it feels."

Rosanna removed the crystal stopper from the vial and poured one drop, for only one drop would come at a time, onto her tongue. She closed her eyes as the liquid filled her mouth and her whole body with warmth. She felt she was a beam of light flashing off the surface of a lake, and she felt she was the lake too. The sensation passed in a moment and left her feeling strong and happy. She opened her eyes.

"Use it only in times of absolute need, and it will last you a lifetime. You can use it for yourself and for any others in great trouble as you choose. It is like the drops from the panther's mouth you witnessed before. The vial and its tiny chain are invisible to everyone but you, so you can wear it round your neck without having to explain. There it will give you unusual insight and comfort. When you put it aside, you will feel as others feel. Both feelings are important to you."

Glinn stood and opened her delicate, blue gown. She stepped forwards and wrapped it around Rosanna. The scent of many flowers filled the air, like the fields of *Grasse* that her grandmother had once described to her. She saw them now in a flash. She wondered at the vision and at the same time felt she never wanted this embrace to end. As Glinn unfolded her from her robe and stepped back, Rosanna heard a faint crackling.

"Remember, I can always hear you if you call out for help. I will send you what you need. You can also visit me by the way Owl has shown you if you have a special need. For now, farewell Rosanna."

"Thank you so very much for this wonderful gift, Glinn. I will protect it and use it only in greatest need."

Feeling full and happy, Rosanna turned on one foot, walked to the far end of the room, turned to wave goodbye and trotted quickly down the stairs to the still-meditating wizard. He opened his eyes as her foot touched the last step.

"I see you received a gift from Glinn. It's very beautiful."

"You can see it? She said others couldn't. People, that is."

His eye sparkled. "Yes. Shall we return?"

He opened his midnight-blue gown. She stepped inside and again they flew through open space the same way they'd come, back through the stars, past the rings of Saturn, past Mars and the moon, until they landed in his room, where Owl sat perched above the table.

"Oh Owl, I've met the most wonderful woman, more than a woman. She was all light and…."

"Yes," said Owl, "she of whom you dreamt but didn't yet know when I found you sitting at your window. I see she gave you a gift."

"Yes, for healing. I don't know how to thank you and Merú. Merú, your name sounds like a call I might make to a bird. Are you to be my teacher too?"

"Yes, now that you know the way through the tree and the clouds, yes. You can come to me any time just as you can travel to Glinn, depending on your need, especially when you are older and have other troubles. We can all help you."

Rosanna rushed forwards to embrace him, kissed his blue, starry-robed belly and spun towards Owl. "Thank you both!"

The door swung open without a sound. Owl sprang from his perch and flew through it and down the stairway. Rosanna walked quickly to the door, turned for a moment to wave goodbye and saw the wizard's eyes twinkling as they had when they first met, only this time she giggled.

"Goodbye Merú!"

She ran out the door and down the stairs with a quick steady beat. She found Owl already nestled on the carpet of cloud. She leapt confidently onto it, and they wove their way down between the other clouds until they came to the very bud from which she had popped out on the twig. She shrank and went into the bud and down the twig to the branch and down the branch into the trunk until she emerged from the wide hole and onto the grass among the tree's exposed roots. Owl swooped down and landed beside her.

"This tree is your door to the other worlds, Rosanna. From it you can go anywhere. Till now, I've taken you from your field, from a path and from your window. Soon, you will be able to go without me, but first I want to show you a couple more things that will help."

"Owl, you're not going to leave me!?"

"No, I'm not going to leave you. You can always call me. But I'm going to show you how to explore on your own and to find me whenever you wish. Don't' worry."

"All these creatures and spirits I'm meeting: are they all really you?" she asked.

"Good question, but no. Each one is unique, and each one has something particular to show you or give you. As your first guide, I can help you find the right one when you ask."

"Now, hop on. Our journey is finished only when I bring you back to where we started."

Rosanna shrank and leapt onto Owl's back. They flew from the hill with Grandmother Thorn and the fairy ring, over the forest and landed back on Rosanna's open window sill. She hopped off and grew back to her normal size. Warmth passed between her and Owl. He swivelled his head towards her, blinked once and leapt from the window sill and away into the sunlit air. Rosanna fingered the little crystal vial hanging from her neck. She thought she might use its nectar on Rachel and Jenny but then remembered Glinn's words. She knew she should use it only in greatest need when no other solution worked. She wondered about what other solution might present itself now.

Chapter Six – Tricky

Rosanna skipped along a path just to the south of her grandparent's cottage. She stopped by a stream and fingered the vial hanging from the delicate chain around her neck. For days she had felt its warmth in her chest, yet she never opened it as she remembered Glinn's instructions. She also tested whether anyone else could see it. She tried her parents first. When she cooked with her father, it hung plainly in sight. She asked him questions about a sauce they were making, so he would have to look straight at her. She even let it bump against her mother while they were bringing in the shopping. Neither one of them noticed it.

Rachel and Jenny, each normally quick to see the slightest addition to her clothing, especially accessories, said nothing when she was with them at separate times. A smile flickered over her grandmother's face once when she seemed to look straight at it, but she said nothing. She often smiled like that when she looked at her granddaughter. Her grandfather jerked his head sideways and glanced at it when she came into his study but he said nothing. He couldn't really see it; no one could. It was hers only and she prized it above everything.

While she fingered the vial with these thoughts, she heard the familiar whoosh of Owl as he landed and perched on an oak limb just across a little stream. "Oh Owl, I'm so glad to see you. I love the vial Glinn gave to me. I wear it all the time."

"Have you opened it?" his eyes narrowed.

"No, because she said only in greatest need."

"Whoo. And you will have need of it one day. You or someone dear to you."

"It makes my chest warm and I feel powerful when I wear it. I know I need to take it off sometimes, but I love the way it makes me feel. Glinn is so very good to give it to me."

"Glinn is perfectly good. That's true. And I still see the stars in your eyes from your visit. Yet I see something else. There's trouble in your eyes again. Do you want to tell me about it?"

"Oh Owl, my two dear friends are fighting worse than ever. They can hardly stand to be in the same room, and their dislike of each other poisons the air. Now they're each trying to turn me against the other. I wish I could do something to change how they feel. I've tried using my influence invisibly, especially after all I've learned, but nothing I try has any effect, and I can't use the elixir. I think there *is* a remedy but I don't see it. It's all such a mess!"

"Whoo hoo. Sometimes you need to take another view of problems you can't solve. I want you to meet a spirit who works in a strange way, very different from the others you've met. He might give you a fresh view of the problem."

Rosanna felt a shudder run through her body, starting from her stomach. "Is he dangerous? Where are you taking me?"

"No, not dangerous. There *are* bad spirits, but you'll not be meeting any of them. No, the spirits you will meet are all good, and they know everything. They can be tricky, but the tricky ones can also help you to see freshly. That's why I want you to meet Coyote. Come, let's pay him a visit."

Holding the vial tight in her left hand for assurance, Rosanna shrank and hopped onto Owl's back. Off they flew high over the forest until they came to the hill of the fairy ring and the old Whitethorn tree. They landed.

"Grandmother Thorn!" Rosanna cried out.

"Yes, you can always come to her to travel. She is a door of going and a door of return. Later, I'll teach you how to come to her on your own. Whenever you arrive, you first greet her, ask permission and then go into the big hole in her trunk. From there you can go anywhere."

She walked up to the tree. "Hello Grandmother Thorn. It's me, Rosanna. I've come to travel to one of the other worlds. May I enter through you?"

The tree creaked and the knothole seemed to grow larger, or did Rosanna shrink? She knew she had been given permission, so she placed her hands on the worn rounded edges of the opening, put her head in, looked down and plunged.

"Curious. Last time I went up; now I'm going downwards. I don't know why but it feels right. Perhaps the Grandmother Thorn knows and is sending me the right way. I must ask Owl later."

As she thought these thoughts, she slid quickly down a tunnel whose roof and sides were ribbed as before when she went up. Down through sudden turns and dips, down, down, until she landed gently on her feet in a cavern. Its floor was a huge slab of stone, and she heard the sound of water in the distance. She felt the presence of others but could not see them.

Owl landed beside her. "Here's one of the places you can always find me. From here we need to go to another place far away. It won't take long to get there as you've learned. Hop on."

They flew through a different tunnel out into the open blue sky. In a few seconds, they glided over an ocean at great speed, close to the surface. In the distance, she saw a whale break water and send a plume of spray into the air, leaving a rainbow in its mist. She laughed as she remembered the rainbow from another adventure. They zoomed past and came to the edge of a huge land. They flew over mountains and plains until they came to a dry, scrubby place full of small shiny red-bark trees and sage. Owl landed next to a boulder at the base of a tall cliff. Rosanna hopped off and grew to her full size. She looked at Owl quizzically.

"Wait just a moment and you'll see," Owl hooted gently as he flapped up onto a large boulder.

From the corner of her eye, she saw a four-legged creature skulk along the cliff wall and slink behind another boulder. Then it peeked around its edge at her. It seemed to be smiling, or was that a snarl? She couldn't tell.

"Come out Coyote," Owl called. The coyote came from behind the boulder, then slid around behind another and, with lowered head, peeked out to look at Rosanna and then quickly ducked away.

"Is he always like this?"

"It's his character. Watch him closely. He won't hurt you."

Rosanna stood and faced the spot where the head had disappeared until the creature very slowly came out, about three skips away. He raised his head and looked into her eyes. Then his head dropped and he seemed to laugh, his mouth open slightly and the corners turned up.

"Who are you? Can you help me with my problem? Will you answer me?" Rosanna didn't feel afraid. She felt annoyed. She felt she wanted to take a hold of this creature and shake him.

The coyote leapt into the air in a back flip and landed on his feet. He stood up on his hind legs and started a little dance, stepping one foot in front of the other and then back. Then the other forwards and back. He swayed his hips from side to side and bobbed his head while he danced. He also moved closer to her. Still, she stood her

ground and faced him.

"Answer me. How can I bring my two fighting friends back together?"

The coyote dropped back down onto all four paws and quickly darted behind her. Before she could react, he jumped onto her shoulders and back.

He was almost weightless. He placed his head on top of her head and it melted down over hers. The two heads merged into one so the coyote's head remained while her own head disappeared. His body clung to her back like a cape. She could see all this as though she were standing a little distance away and watching. There she stood, a girl's body with the head of a coyote. She started to giggle; it looked and felt so funny. Her laugh came barking out as she started stepping from side to side, and her arms moved in wavy, snake-like shapes. Her head filled with all sorts of disruptive thoughts – turning over a table full of food at home, tying Tamara's shoe laces together in the cloak room during sports period, snatching the teacher's purse and running off with it, stealing pears from a neighbour's tree, telling a lie to her mother, making mischief in every corner of her life. It was like a dream at high speed.

She danced over to Owl. "You fat, squat thing! It's a wonder you can fly. You're impossible," she barked and danced away again. She dropped to her hands and knees and crawled around a boulder, where she crouched and hid from Owl, laughing.

"Enough!" she shouted from inside the coyote's head. "Let me go!" Quick as that, the coyote's head slid away from her own. The creature hopped off her shoulders and onto the ground behind her. She turned to see him lope over to Owl, where he sat down and faced her. He was smiling and Owl swivelled his head from left to right. For an instant, the two figures slid into each other. She could see both even though they were in the same place. Then they slid apart.

"What is going on here Owl? This foolish creature makes me want to turn everything on its head. And he keeps sliding in and out of others."

"Any answer you get from this one will be a riddle, a trick, perhaps just a silly dance. He doesn't talk. He dances and makes you a little crazy. Quite different from Glinn, yes?

The coyote was snickering again but didn't move. Rosanna walked over to him and looked into his narrowed eyes. Then, as though a dusty old blanket was shaken out, she had a clear thought.

"I don't need to 'fix' anything between Rachel and Jennie," Rosanna thought." "I'd do better if I just played with them like Coyote, if I 'danced' with them. I don't need a magic spell or a potion." Owl and Coyote could see these thoughts dance in her eyes.

Quick as a cat, the coyote leapt towards her, slipped a forepaw under her arm and twirled her around once. Her hair whipped straight out from the speed of it. She caught her balance and her breath as the coyote slipped away behind a boulder and vanished.

"Hoo, that's how it goes with him. Something curious always happens, but you're not quite sure what it means. You may understand in a twinkling or maybe a few days later. Keep Coyote with you and remember how you felt when your two heads melted together. In future, you'll know when to call Coyote."

Owl ambled sideways towards her and Rosanna shrank. It was time to go. She didn't even have a moment to say goodbye. They flew at full speed over the great land, past the shore and over the ocean where again she saw the whale break the surface and again saw the rainbow in its mist. They dived into the tunnel, flew back to the cavern and landed. Rosanna hopped down from Owl's back.

"You always return the way you went out so that you gather up all yourself from the journey. Now go back through the tunnel that brought you here, up to the large opening in Grandmother Thorn's trunk."

Rosanna made a little leap and flew up into the ribbed tunnel, slid along the turns and sudden rises, until she popped out through the opening into the full light of the sun. Owl was there, ready to take her home. She jumped onto his back and they flew over the forest and back to the path and the stream where they met.

"Thank you for taking me to Coyote, Owl," she said. "He helped me to see my problem in a completely different way. I don't have to choose between my two friends. Still, I do want to bring them together."

"You mean choose between both your different sides *and* your different kinds of friends?"

"Well, yes, both! Oh I feel much better now."

"That *is* good. Next, you need just one more important helper so you can travel to Grandmother Thorn and beyond whenever you wish. Meanwhile, go enjoy your friends and see how their difference is ok.

A few days later during lunch break at school, Rosanna was sitting with Rachel having a quiet chat. In the corner of her eye, she saw Jenny sitting at distance watching them, but Rosanna didn't let on she saw her. Rachel made a funny remark about a gawky English teacher, and Rosanna responded by doing a coyote dance on the spot, mimicking the man. She stood up and bobbed her head as Otter and did a snake dance with her arms as Coyote, and she tapped her feet all in imitation of the poor teacher. She looked a complete fool, yet she captured exactly what Rachel described. This caused both her friends to giggle at the same time and then break into full laughter till they cried as she danced. When they both caught their breath again and opened their eyes, their eyes met. Something friendly passed between them, a mixture of wicked wit and love for their friend, Rosanna. Jenny quickly looked away, embarrassed by the glance, but Rosanna could see she was still smiling. When she looked at Rachel, she saw a blush just starting to fade from her cheeks and a little smile.

"Rosanna," she said, "you got him in a heartbeat."

Nothing more happened and lunch ended, but Rosanna saw the good humour pass between her two friends. She felt perhaps that there was hope that they might be friends again after all.

"Ah, leave it to Coyote," she thought.

Chapter Seven – Spirit of the Drum

Rosanna stood in the middle of the meadow that stretches far beyond her grandparents' cottage in the Wicklow mountains. She brimmed with memories of her adventures with Owl – their first meeting and flight, their visit to the flower, encounters with Otter and Panther, Glinn and Merú high in the sky, and the antics of that tricky Coyote. Still, she knew there was something more, something she needed that was missing, full and happy as she might feel now.

"Owl," she called barely above a whisper. "Can you come now?"

A moment's silence and then the whoosh of wings and his soft landing. Owl stood before her and looked into her eyes. He understood what she wanted. His voice spoke in her mind.

"You remember Grandmother Thorn, whose opening you entered to go up to Merú and Glinn, whose opening you used to go down into the lower world and travel to Coyote?" He knew she remembered; he was leading her.

"That is your door from this world to the other worlds, from ordinary to non-ordinary reality. Till now, you've waited for me to take you to someone or to the tree and beyond. Now I want to show you how to travel to that door and beyond on your own. There is another spirit you need to meet."

"But Owl, you promised you wouldn't leave me?" Rosanna protested for the second time since they met.

"No, I'm going to show you how you can find me whenever you wish. But let's slow down and back up to remember something. Do you recall the sound of Otter's steps when you danced with him and do you remember Panther's footsteps when you ran together, that steady badababump? You heard it again as you trotted up the steps to Merú and Glinn. It's like the regular tum tum tum of a drum that carried you along. It's like your heartbeat. That's the key to your travelling from now on, this steady beat. The beating of a drum will be your magic carpet to anywhere."

Rosanna's eyes widened as Owl spoke. Owl's eyes narrowed. "Never mind for now how it works. You'll learn soon enough. Before that, I want to show you how the first drum was born, so when you have your own, you'll know how it came to be. Hop on and let's go."

She shrank, leapt onto Owl's back and off they shot towards Grandmother Thorn. They landed and paused so Rosanna could greet the old tree. Then she slid into the opening, went up through the trunk and out a limb into a branch, and finally she popped out through the tip of a twig, where Owl waited for her to land on his back. Up they flew at great speed straight into open space, past the moon and huge asteroids, past all the planets until they came to a great open darkness where stars twinkled in the distance. She could see the ragged, feathery edge of something huge. It looked like cloth.

"Owl, what is this?"

"This is the edge of the First Drum. I want you to hear her story directly from her. Don't be frightened by her size. Her voice will sound in your mind as mine does." When Owl finished, the feathery edge turned and Rosanna saw a gigantic round surface of stretched material. She couldn't say what it was made of, but it gave off its own light.

"What are you? Who are you?" The words came before she could think of anything else to say. A low-pitched feminine voice sounded in her head.

"At the beginning of our galaxy, I was an invisible spirit, magnetic and tense with energy. I attracted the nearby star dust to me, and it gathered into my shape until I became visible, stretched across space, firm and impassable: the First Drum. Asteroids big and small flew against me in a steady stream. The sound of their hitting filled space with a new voice, my voice. I gave sound to the flowing movement of our galaxy. I became the pulse at the centre of everything, even the Earth.

"Your earliest people could hear this beat. They called it the earth's heartbeat and they made round shapes with stretched skin to echo my sound. They used these drums to move through different layers of their world and through time. They learned to see invisible spirits and to talk with them for information about their lives and for healing when they became ill. I am the mother of those early drums and all the drums that have come after. I can carry you wherever you need to go when you have questions that need answers. Now go receive your own drum and, through it, learn my ways."

Rosanna sat still on Owl's back while they hovered in space. She listened deeply to the boom, boom, boom of the drum as huge solid rocks flew against it and bounced away. She closed her eyes, put her hand to her chest and felt her own heartbeat echoing the beat of this huge drum.

Owl made a gentle turn and started back to Earth. Knowing the importance of what she had seen, he stayed silent and left Rosanna to her thoughts. They returned to the same twig, and she melted into it and moved down into a branch, into a limb, into the trunk and out the opening onto the grass beside the old Thorn. She walked to the centre of the fairy ring and stared across the valley. She remembered the sound of the drum beat in space and listened for its echo from the earth. "I'm just imagining it," she thought.

"Don't dismiss your imagination," said Owl, who had settled beside her. "You use it for all our adventures. How else could you see me, go with me, talk to Otter, Panther, Coyote and Drum? If you ignore it, you cut off one of your senses. I'm here to teach you that, Rosanna, and the drum is Nature's gift so that you have your own magic carpet. Now, it's time you received your first drum."

Rosanna stood to face Owl, for she knew something important was going to happen. She heard a sound tumbling, rumbling, bounding down a distant hill.

"There."

Owl pointed towards the hill beside them. She could see the speck of it rolling like a small boulder down the hillside. It rolled into the floor of the valley and up the hill towards her at speed. Wondrous as this was, she had the wit to reach out at the last second and catch it as it flew, snap, into her hands. Her own drum!!

She turned it over and felt its skin on one face and the rope tendrils for gripping it on the back face. She gripped these and held the drum before her, a little wider than the length of her forearm. She thought it was humming.

"Later, you will find a beater, but for now use your thumb to beat a steady rhythm against it." She gripped the tendrils and tilted the edge of the drum towards her head and began to tap a steady beat with the edge of her thumb. She lifted it closer to her face and leaned her ear towards its skin. From the centre of the beat, a bubble of sound grew around her head. It sounded like a choir of voices, "Ahhhh."

"It's singing for you," Owl observed. "It's saying hello." Rosanna smiled and whispered her private words of greeting into the drum's skin. She continued beating until she forgot about Owl and her surroundings. She felt herself flying up into the warm afternoon air, free and happy.

Slowly she settled back down to the ground and stopped tapping. She pressed the drum skin to her chest.

"Thank you Owl," she sang in gratitude. "Thank you for this wonderful gift."

"It is your birthright to own it and use it. Come, we need to connect some dots in your adventures. Say goodbye to your tree and we'll go back to the meadow."

Rosanna faced the old Thorn and, keeping her eyes on the opening, made a respectful bow. Then she and her drum shrank as she hopped onto Owl's back and they flew back to her meadow. They landed and Rosanna hopped off Owl's back and settled herself on a flat stone with her drum.

"I want to tell you how to use the drum. From any place, not just this meadow or your grandparents' cottage, you can use the drum to carry you to Grandmother Thorn. First, think of what you want to learn or find. Say it to yourself three times. Then start to tap the drum in a steady rhythm at a pace that feels right to you. You'll find your own speed. Close your eyes and picture Grandmother Thorn. Picture yourself there and greet her. This is your starting point. Decide whether you want to go upwards towards Merú and Glinn or down towards our cavern, where I'll meet you. Over time, you'll find other guides to help you."

"Still steadily drumming the whole time, when you arrive at either place, upperworld or lowerworld, ask your question or make your request again. I or another will take you to where you need to go. Remember the exact path you travel because you'll need to return the same way. When you have what you need, stop drumming for a moment. Pause and then make a few slow beats. Then bring yourself all the way back with a quicker beat – quick, quick – as you retrace your path at high speed until you come back out at the opening of Grandmother Thorn. Then stop your drumming. You always start and return at the same place, so you never get lost but come home safely.

Rosanna listened to everything with her chin resting on the rim of the drum. "I can't wait to try," she said. "Up till now, you've made travel easy for me. Will travelling with the drum be so easy?"

"Not always. You need to be in the right mood and in strong need of an answer. The more you use your drum, the better it works to carry you wherever you need to go. I'll always try to meet you, but I might be busy sometimes." His eyes narrowed in the way of a smile.

"One other thing: you need a beater. You can make one out of a stick with a tight cloth ball at the end. Perhaps your grandfather will help you get a proper mallet. Ask him. But then you will have to tell him why. That should be curious."

"Oh I think he'd understand. He's funny that way. He might even approve of our adventures if I tell him about them."

"As you wish, Rosanna. Now I must leave until you want me again. Use the drum to call me. There's plenty more for us to explore. See you again soon."

With a single leap, Owl took off and flew in great spirals higher and higher until he disappeared. She gazed over the meadow with her drum under her arm. She was thinking about how long ago it was that they first met.

"Yes, Owl. Soon."

Acknowledgements

I would like to thank Simon Buxton and Naomi Lewis for their years of guidance in the journey and their encouragement to make stories.

A special thanks to my sister, Kathy Forster for her aesthetics and her drawings. How well you imagined these stories. Also to Lauren Forster for her graphics contribution.

Among my adult readers who have so helpfully advised me, thanks to Marianne Jacuzzi, Peter Weltner, Tony Mulqueen, Catherine Gaynor, and Abby Wynne.

Abby, thanks for helping me launch this jewel into the world.

Among my pre-adult readers, thanks to Ava Jacuzzi, Maya Mulhearn, Dylan and Spencer Thomas, and Mya Wynne for your intelligent readings.

About the Author: Robert Mohr, Ph.D.

Robert began shamanic studies in 2003 under Simon Buxton and Naomi Lewis of The Sacred Trust in the UK and completed an intensive two-year training as a shamanic practitioner in 2008. He has taught writing skills for years to both children and adults and worked professionally as an instructional designer. In 1998, he published How to Write: Tools for the Craft (UCD Press, Dublin).

When his first granddaughter was born, he envisioned teaching her how to use her imagination to seek answers to life's questions. He searched through his own journal of shamanic journeys for this series of adventures, which teach some basic methods of the journey along the way. Rosanna's adventures open this ancient practice to her and to all children.

About the Illustrator: Kathleen Mohr Forster

Kathleen has taught art to college students and teenagers for the past four decades in San Francisco, Salt Lake City (Utah) and Orlando (Florida), all the time working as an active fine artist in painting, etching, drawings and silkscreen. She has a BFA in Fine Arts and Humanities and an MFA in both illustration and Fine Art. Her artwork has been shown and collected by galleries and private collectors worldwide. She applies her years of experience and a magical eye to the illustrations for Rosanna and Owl.

24794752R00045

Printed in Poland
by Amazon Fulfillment
Poland Sp. z o.o., Wrocław